# Contents

# A Monster
# Ate My Marmite

## by

## Eric Brown

## Illustrated by Shona Grant

To Freya, with love

First published in 2011 in Great Britain by
Barrington Stoke Ltd
18 Walker St, Edinburgh, EH3 7LP

www.barringtonstoke.co.uk

ISBN: 978-1-84299-111-4

Printed in China by Leo

# Chapter 1
# Umba-Wumba!

I was walking down the lane with my best friend Millie. I had been to the shop, and I had a jar of Marmite in my bag. I wanted to get home and make a big Marmite sandwich.

It was Friday, and I was thinking about our home-work. We had to write a story about knights in armour.

"I have a great idea," Millie said. "You can do the home-work with me. We'll make up a story tomorrow."

"But I don't have any books about knights," I said.

"I've got lots of books at home," Millie said. "We can write a great story about knights and dragons and fairy-tale castles!"

I smiled at Millie. "But dragons and fairy-tale castles weren't real!"

"How do you know, Mouse? Maybe they were real, just like knights and kings and princesses."

I heard a loud cry from behind us. "Millie! Mouse!"

In the field near the lane was a silver space-ship. "It's Umba-Wumba's space-time ship!" Millie said.

"And there's Umba-Wumba!" I yelled.

He was sitting on the wall like Humpty-Dumpty. He waved at us.

We ran to our alien friend. He jumped off the wall and bounced up and down. Umba-Wumba was round and orange, and had an eye at the end of his long nose. He hugged us with his four arms.

"It's great to see you again, Millie and Mouse!" he said.

"And it's great to see you," Millie said.

Umba-Wumba held our hands and took us to his space-time ship. "I'm taking you on a trip in time!" he said. "Where would you like to go?"

I looked at Millie. She said, "Perhaps we could go back to the Middle Ages, to the time of knights in armour and dragons and fairy-tale castles."

I said, "Can you take us back to the year 1400, Umba-Wumba?"

"Yes I can," he said, bouncing up and down. "But are you sure you don't want to go further back in time, to the time of the dinosaurs?" He smiled at us.

Last year, Umba-Wumba took us to the time of the dinosaurs in his space-time ship. Dinosaurs had run after us and almost eaten us.

"No thank you!" Millie said.

"We never want to go there again," I said. "I think the year 1400 will be very nice, thank you."

We ran into the field to Umba-Wumba's space-time ship and walked up the ramp.

4

# Chapter 2
# Back In Time

We sat down on two chairs in the space-time ship. Umba-Wumba stood near the controls and pressed buttons with his four hands. Soon the ship began to shake and rattle. I held on tight.

I looked out of the window. The green field was gone. I could see just a grey blur.

"Look," Millie said. She pointed to a screen on the wall, full of numbers. It was the date: 2011.

I looked hard at the numbers, and suddenly they moved.

2000 ... 1950 ... 1900 ... 1800 ...

We were moving faster and faster as we went back in time.

"Soon we'll be there!" Millie yelled. "In the time of knights and dragons!"

The screen said: 1700 ... 1600 ... 1500 ...

Umba-Wumba pressed a button and the space-time ship stopped rattling.

The screen said: 1400.

I looked out of the window. We were in a forest. All I could see were green trees.

"Now let's go out and have a look around," Umba-Wumba said.

We held his hands and walked to the door. He pressed a button and the door slid open. We walked down the ramp and stood in the forest.

"It's just like the woods near where we live," Millie told Umba-Wumba.

The round little alien bounced along in front of us. We ran after him. Soon we came to a path that led into the trees. We walked down the path. It was a lovely sunny day. The sound of birds singing filled the air.

In front of us, Umba-Wumba stopped. He pointed to a tree and we hid behind it. "Look," he said, pointing.

We looked around the tree. We could see a small village.

A group of people stood in front of the tiny houses. They were shouting at each other.

"I wonder what the problem is?" Millie said.

# Chapter 3
# A Dirty Knight

"Look at the houses," Millie said. "They're tiny, and almost falling down."

The houses looked like small wooden boxes and they had big holes in the walls. Skinny pigs and thin goats rooted around in the mud in front of the houses. The people looked like they needed a good meal, too. They were as thin as the goats, and were dressed in rags.

"What a stink!" I said.

Millie held her nose. A nasty smell came from the village.

Umba-Wumba said, "The people of this time are very poor, Millie. They don't have toilets in their houses."

Millie stared at our alien friend. "But where do they poo?"

Umba-Wumba waved his long nose. "They do it outside, in their gardens. Then the pigs eat it."

"No!" Millie said. "That's yucky!"

"These people don't have a lot of money, Millie. They farm the little bit of land they have, and they keep a few pigs and goats and chickens. But when the harvest is bad, they don't have a lot to eat. Some people even die from hunger."

Millie shook her head. She looked sad. She pointed to the men and women. "I wonder what the problem is?"

A group of ten people were shouting at a tall boy.

"Why can't you do anything about it?" a man yelled at the boy.

"We pay you to look after us," a woman said.

"And you call yourself a knight!" said a man.

The boy said, "How would you like to fight a monster as big as a house?"

The people standing round him started to shout again. Someone even threw a bad apple at the boy.

Millie was shaking her head. "But knights should be tall and brave, in silver armour …"

"I think this one is a rather poor knight," Umba-Wumba said.

"Look at his armour!" I said. "It looks like two bits of dust-bin lid! He looks like a scarecrow, not a knight!"

A man with a big nose said, "Now go away! And don't come back until you've killed the monster!"

The tall boy hung his head and walked away from the village. "Hide," Umba-Wumba said. "He's coming this way!"

We ducked behind the tree.

# Chapter 4
# The Monster!

The knight walked past us, and then stopped. He turned and looked hard at us.

He was about 16, very thin and very dirty. His nose was running and he looked like he hadn't had a bath in years. He had bits of rotten apple in his dirty hair.

Millie whispered to me, "Mouse – he smells!"

"A real knight in shining armour!" I said.

"And who are you?" said the knight. Then he saw Umba-Wumba. "What is this! Are you a devil, sir? Are you a goblin?"

Umba-Wumba jumped up and down. "No! I'm not a goblin or a devil!"

"Then you must be a monster," said the knight. He held a long sword, and he pointed it at our alien friend. *Oh no*, I said to myself, *he's going to kill Umba-Wumba!*

Millie yelled, "No! He's not a monster!"

I said, "No, he's our very good friend."

The knight looked at us. "A boy and a girl – in strange clothing. Are you friends of this turnip-head?"

I tried not to smile. Millie said, "He's not a turnip-head. His name is Umba-Wumba."

The knight looked at Umba-Wumba, then at Millie and me. "And what are you doing in this wood?" he asked. "Have you not heard of the evil beast?"

"The evil beast?" I said. I grabbed hold of Millie's hand. "What evil beast, sir?"

Millie looked excited. "Is it a dragon?"

"I don't think so," the knight said. "I haven't seen the beast. It lives not far from here, in a cave. The people in the village say it's a monster."

"A monster!" I yelled. "You mean, monsters are real?"

"As real as you and me," said the knight.

"So there really are monsters!" Millie said. "And it might be a dragon!"

The knight wiped his runny nose on the back of his hand, and stood up proudly. "And I'm going to slay the monster!"

Millie looked hard at the knight. "Slay the monster?" she said.

The knight shook his sword. "With this very sword!" he said.

"But why?" Millie said. She was looking very sad. Millie didn't like people who were cruel to animals – or to monsters.

The knight said, "Last week, the evil beast came to the village. It knocked over houses and nearly squashed five people."

"Was anyone hurt?" Millie asked.

"One man had a broken leg," the knight said. "And everyone was very frightened. They told me about the beast, so I have come to kill it!"

Umba-Wumba said, "Can we come with you, sir?"

The knight nodded. "Of course. It is only a short way to the monster's cave. You can watch me kill the beast. Then you can tell the people in the village how brave I am! Follow me!"

The knight strode along the path. We followed him.

Millie whispered to Umba-Wumba, "But I don't want to see the knight kill the monster, even if the monster is an evil beast."

Umba-Wumba said, "It's OK, Millie. I'll make sure the knight doesn't kill the monster."

# Chapter 5
# The Useless Knight

We came to the end of the forest. In front of us were fields, and then big hills.

The knight pointed at the hills. "That is where the monster lives. Follow me."

The knight walked across the fields and we went after him. Soon we came to the hills. In the side of a hill was a dark cave.

"In there," the knight whispered.

I looked hard, but the cave was very dark. "I don't see anything," I said.

Umba-Wumba said, "Maybe the monster has gone out to do what monsters do."

"No!" Millie said suddenly. "I can hear something. Listen."

We listened. The sound of very loud snoring seemed to be coming from inside the cave.

"The monster is asleep," I said.

Umba-Wumba said to the knight, "You can't kill the monster when it's asleep! That's not fair!"

"But it will be a lot better than trying to kill it when it's awake," said the knight.

I looked at the bits of rusty tin he wore on his chest. "What kind of knight are you, anyway? I thought all knights were strong and brave?"

"I am strong and brave," the knight said in a soft voice. "Only ..."

"Only what?" Millie said.

"Well, how would you feel if you had to kill a monster?" the knight said. "I mean, have you ever seen a monster? The people in the village said that this one is evil – with big ears and long teeth and a great long nose. And monsters love to gobble up knights!" the knight said with a moan.

"Listen," Umba-Wumba said.

We heard another sound coming from inside the cave. The snoring had stopped.

"Oh, no!" Millie said. "The monster is waking up! If it's a dragon, it will come out and roast us with its fire!"

23

I heard a loud snort as the monster woke up. Then I heard footsteps like thunder as the monster stomped around in its cave.

"Run," the knight said, "before the beast eats us!"

We ran back down the hill, into the forest, and hid behind a tree.

We looked back at the cave, but the monster was not coming out. We sat down on the grass behind the tree.

"Now I've got to kill the monster when it is awake," the knight said. "What will I do if it eats me?"

"Maybe you shouldn't kill it," Millie said. "Maybe you should just go home and forget about the monster."

"But then the people in the village wouldn't give me food."

"Can't you do anything else?" Millie said. "Like jousting?"

I looked at Millie. "What does jousting mean?"

Millie laughed. "Oh, Mouse, you are a dim-wit! Jousting is when two knights fight with long lances, and try to knock each other off their horses."

"Well," said the knight in a soft voice, "I did try jousting once, but I fell off my horse and hurt my head."

I tried not to giggle. We had found the most useless knight in England! He wasn't brave at all.

"Well, why don't you go to war and fight for the King?" Millie said.

The knight shook his head. "I don't like the idea of that," he said. "I might get killed."

"Just what kind of knight are you?" I said.

The knight looked unhappy. "A bad one," he said.

Umba-Wumba said, "But why did you become a knight in the first place?"

"It's a long story," said the knight in rusty armour. "Would you like to hear it?"

"Yes please!" said Millie.

# Chapter 6
# The Knight's Story

"You see," said the knight, "my father was a brave knight. He fought in wars and was good at jousting. He even saved damsels in distress."

I looked at Millie. "What's a damsel?" I asked. "And what does distress mean?"

Millie laughed at me. "A damsel is a lady, and distress means in trouble. Knights liked to save ladies. It made the knights feel good."

Umba-Wumba said to the boy, "What happened to your father?"

"Well, one day he was jousting with another knight – and he got knocked off his horse and died."

"Oh, no," said Millie. "I'm sorry. Do you live with your mother now?"

The knight shook his head. "My mother died when I was five," he said. "I live alone in a hut in the woods."

"But why did you become a knight?" Umba-Wumba asked.

The knight smiled sadly. "I wanted to be like my father," he said. "The trouble is, I don't have much armour – just what I'm wearing. I don't even have a helmet! Also," the knight went on, "I'm not very brave. In fact, I'm useless."

"Mmm ..." said Umba-Wumba. He looked at the boy with the eye on the end of his nose. "I have an idea."

I looked at our orange alien friend. "What kind of idea?" I asked.

"I think I can get rid of the monster, so that it doesn't attack the village."

The knight smiled happily. "Can you do that?"

Umba-Wumba waved his nose. "Of course I can!"

Millie looked hard at Umba-Wumba. "You're not going to kill it, are you?"

Umba-Wumba laughed. "Of course not, Millie. I'm going to talk to the monster!"

He moved from behind the tree and bounced up the hill to the monster's cave.

# Chapter 7
# The Monster Talks

The knight ran after Umba-Wumba.
I took Millie's hand and we walked up the hill.

We stopped in front of the cave. There
was no sound from inside. "Perhaps it's
asleep again," said the knight.

"I don't hear it snoring," Millie said.

Umba-Wumba said, "OK. I'm going into
the cave now. I'll talk to the monster. I'll tell

him that there is a knight outside who wants to kill him. But I'll say that I have a better idea."

"What is it?" I asked.

"I will ask the monster if it will come with me in my space-time ship," Umba-Wumba said. "Then I'll take it away from here to a safe place."

"And the people in the village will think that the knight killed the monster," Millie said. She looked at the knight. "You'll be a hero!"

The knight smiled. "I just hope Umba-Wumba's plan works," he said.

"Right," said Umba-Wumba. "I'm going into the cave."

"Be careful, Umba-Wumba," Millie said. She held my hand.

Umba-Wumba bounced into the cave. I watched him go. Soon I couldn't see him in the dark shadows.

"I hope the monster doesn't eat him," the knight said.

"Umba-Wumba can bounce very fast!" I said. "The monster won't eat him."

Millie pulled me behind some rocks. The knight came with us. We sat down and waited.

Soon we heard a noise from in the cave. It was a loud huffing and puffing. "That must be the monster," I said.

We heard more puffing and huffing. "And that's Umba-Wumba," I said. "I didn't know he could speak monster!"

Suddenly more noises came from the cave. These noises sounded like loud

trumpets. Millie covered her ears with her hands.

"I think that was the monster," the knight said. "I hope it isn't angry with Umba-Wumba."

Umba-Wumba came out of the cave. I stood up and waved, and our alien friend bounced over to us.

"Is the monster chasing you?" Millie asked.

"No," Umba-Wumba said. "He's really very friendly – for a monster."

"But what is he like?" I asked.

Umba-Wumba waved his four hands and his long nose. "The monster is the oddest beast I have ever seen in my life," he said. "It is very fat, with a big head and massive ears."

"But how many legs does it have?" I asked.

"Four – and they're as big as tree trunks," Umba-Wumba said. "It has long teeth sticking out of its mouth, and its nose is like mine, very long. But it doesn't have an eye on the end."

I didn't like the sound of that!

"But did you really talk to the monster?" Millie asked.

"Of course I did, Millie. I can talk to many things – even monsters!"

"But what did you talk about?" I said.

"Oh, I asked where the monster came from, and what it was doing here. I asked it what it liked to eat, and why it had stomped around the village."

"And what did it say?" asked the knight.

"The monster said that it came from a hot country far away. It told me it was trapped by some bad men and taken to England in a cage. It was put in a circus, but it got away and found this cave."

"But why did it attack the people in the village?" the knight asked.

"The monster ran after the people because they came and threw stones at it. And it was looking for food in the village. You see, the monster is always hungry."

"What kind of food does it like?" Millie asked.

"It said it was looking for fruit and grass – but not the kind of grass that grows here."

Suddenly, Millie burst out laughing. "Umba-Wumba, what colour was the monster?"

Umba-Wumba waved his nose. "It was very dark in the cave," he said. "But I think the monster was grey."

"Of course it was!" Millie shouted. "I know what the monster is – and it's not a monster at all."

Before I could stop her, Millie stood up and ran into the cave.

"Come back!" I yelled.

"I'm going after Millie," Umba-Wumba said, and bounced into the cave.

I held my head in my hands. I hoped the monster wouldn't eat Millie!

"For a girl," said the knight, "Millie is very brave."

I nodded. "She's the bravest girl in the world," I said. "And my best friend ... Oh, Millie, what have you done?"

# Chapter 8
# We See the Monster

A moment later, Millie walked out of the cave with Umba-Wumba. She was smiling. I ran to her and gave her a big hug. "You're safe!" I said.

"Of course I'm safe, Mouse."

"But the monster ...?" I began

Millie laughed loudly. "The monster is no monster, Mouse." She shook her head, a little sadly. "There are no dragons, or monsters ..."

"But what is it?" I asked.

Umba-Wumba said, "It's a very hungry animal, Mouse. It asked us if we had any food."

"If it was hungry," I said, "then why didn't it eat you?"

Millie laughed again. "Because these animals don't eat meat," she said.

"It sounds like a very odd animal," I said.

"Oh, Mouse – no! It's not very odd at all. You've seen them at the zoo and on TV. Come and see." She took my hand and tried to drag me into the cave.

"No!" I yelled. "I'm not going!"

Then I stopped and looked at the cave.
Something very big was coming out of the
cave.

"Oh!" I said. "Oh!"

The knight yelled out loud and hid behind a rock. He was shaking so much that his rusty armour rattled.

Millie laughed, and so did I.

Millie was right. The monster was not a monster at all.

It was an elephant!

It stepped from the cave, swinging its trunk. It looked at me with its small eyes. Then it lifted its trunk and made a sound like a trumpet.

Umba-Wumba said, "It wants to know if you have any food, Mouse."

I smiled. "Yes, I have," I said. I opened my bag and pulled out the jar. "But I don't think the elephant will like Marmite!"

I opened the lid and held the jar out to the elephant.

The elephant swung its trunk to the jar and gave a big sniff. Then it snatched the jar with its trunk and lifted it to its mouth.

A great big pink tongue came out of its mouth and slurped up all the Marmite from the jar.

"Oh, Mouse!" Millie shouted. "The elephant ate your Marmite!"

The elephant made a loud trumpet sound.

"And it wants some more!" Umba-Wumba said.

# Chapter 9
# Goodbye Monster

The knight moved from behind the rock and walked up to us. He looked at the elephant with wide eyes.

"But ... but the monster isn't attacking you!" the knight said.

I smiled. "It isn't a monster. It looks funny, but it's very gentle. I've seen lots of elephants in our time."

The knight looked at me. "What do you mean, 'in your time'?" he asked.

Millie said, "You see, we come from the future – six hundred years in the future. We came back in time in Umba-Wumba's space-time machine."

The knight shook his head. "I'm feeling dizzy!" he said.

The elephant trumpeted again.

Umba-Wumba made a loud elephant sound with his little mouth. He turned to us. "The elephant is hungry, but I told it to wait. Soon it will have all the food it can eat."

Millie said, "But where will you take it, Umba-Wumba?"

The little round alien bounced up and down. "I will take it in my space-time ship to the elephant's home in Africa. Then I'll come back here for you, Mouse and Millie."

Umba-Wumba took hold of the elephant's trunk and led it down the hill. We moved into the forest to Umba-Wumba's space-time ship.

"Good-bye, elephant," Millie said. "It was nice to meet you."

"Good-bye," I said. "I hope you have a great time in Africa."

The elephant lifted its trunk and made a loud sound.

Umba-Wumba smiled. "The elephant said, thank you for the Marmite!"

The knight shook one of Umba-Wumba's four hands. "Thank you for taking the monster – I mean the elephant – away from here. The people of the village will be happy that it has gone for ever."

Umba-Wumba and the elephant walked up the ramp. Umba-Wumba waved. "I'll be back soon to take you home, Mouse and Millie."

The door closed, and seconds later the space-time ship vanished.

"Now," Millie said to the knight, "I think we should go to the village and tell everyone that you got rid of the monster!"

# Chapter 10
# A Brave Knight, Really

We walked into the village. I wanted to hold my nose to shut out the bad smell – but that would have been rude.

When the men and women from the village saw the knight, they stopped what they were doing. They pointed to the knight and shouted for their friends to come out of the houses.

Soon a small crowd stood in front of us.

The man with a big nose said, "Well, knight? Did you kill the monster?"

"Yes," said a girl, "will the evil beast attack us again?"

The knight held up his hand. "I can tell you this – the monster has gone! It will never return! You're safe now in the village!"

The man with the big nose looked at me. "Is it true, stranger? Are we safe at last from the monster?"

I nodded. "You're safe. What the knight says is true!"

Everyone cheered. They tossed their hats into the air and danced around. "Hurrah! Hurrah!" they shouted. "Three cheers for the knight!"

"Hip-hip-hurrah!" everyone shouted.

The knight smiled happily.

The man with the big nose stepped up to the knight and handed him a basket of food.

"Thank you for getting rid of the monster," he said. "Now, will you stay with us and save us from any more monsters that might attack us?"

The knight looked nervous. "I need to think about it," he said. "Perhaps I should talk it over with my friends."

We moved away from the crowd, and the knight said, "Well, I could stay here and work as a knight. But what if a real monster came to the village?"

Millie smiled. "Do you know something, knight? I don't think real monsters exist. There are no dragons, or flying beasts – just in fairy-tales."

The knight thought about that and nodded.

I said, "I think you should stay here. You are brave, really."

The knight looked hard at me. "I am?"

"Of course you are," I said. "You've met people from the future, and an orange alien with four arms and an eye at the end of his nose, and you weren't frightened."

The knight smiled. "No. No, I wasn't, was I? Do you know something? I think I will stay here. If I work hard at it, I might become a good knight one day!"

We said good-bye to the knight, and he walked over to the men and women and told them that he would stay.

Everyone cheered when the knight told them the good news. Then we turned to go.

We gave him a wave goodbye and walked into the woods.

We came to the gap among the trees and waited for Umba-Wumba's space-time ship.

Millie was looking a bit sad. "What's wrong?" I asked her.

"Well … do you know something, Mouse? When we came back to 1400, I hoped there would be castles, and kings and queens, and knights in shining armour – and monsters and dragons." She shook her head. "But fairy-tales aren't real, are they?"

I held my friend's hand. "Maybe not," I said. "But our adventures in time are real, Millie! I mean, time-travel with an orange alien is fantastic, isn't it?"

Millie smiled happily. "You're right, Mouse. Of course it is."

Two minutes later, Umba-Wumba's space-time ship landed in front of us. The ramp came down and Umba-Wumba bounced out.

"Is the elephant happy in Africa?" Millie asked.

Umba-Wumba waved his long nose. "Very happy, now that he has plenty of food to eat."

"I wonder if it will miss eating Marmite?" I laughed.

We ran up the ramp into the space-time ship.

# Chapter 11
# Home!

We sat in the seats and Umba-Wumba pressed the buttons.

The ship rattled. The screen on the wall showed the date: 1400 ... 1600 ... then 1700 ...

"We'll soon be home, Mouse," Millie said.

1800 ... 1900 ... 2011.

The ship stopped shaking. Out of the window I could see the green fields, with cows eating the grass.

We moved to the ramp.

"Good-bye, Umba-Wumba," I said. "Thanks for taking us on a great adventure!"

"Bye, Umba-Wumba," Millie said.

We hugged our alien friend.

"Good-bye, Mouse and Millie. I will come and visit you again soon!"

We walked down the ramp, and turned around and watched the space-time ship shoot into the sky. Umba-Wumba stood by the window, waving his four arms.

When the ship had vanished, I said, "Now, I must go to the shop and get some more Marmite! And then we'll do our home-work."

*******

On Monday morning at school I stood up in front of the class.

Mr Brooke said, "Now, Mouse has written a very fanciful story. Does anyone know what 'fanciful' means?"

Millie lifted her hand into the air. "I do! Fanciful means that the story is made up." She giggled to herself. "He made the story up, and it didn't really happen."

"Yes, Millie," Mr Brooke said. "Fanciful means that Mouse has used his imagination to make up this fantastic story. And now he will read it out to you."

All the class looked at me.

"A Monster Ate My Marmite," I said. "I was walking down the lane with my best friend Millie ..."

Barrington Stoke would like to thank all its readers for commenting on the manuscript before publication and in particular:

Harvey Beament
Ricky Black
Asaph Bondo
Carly Burns
Saskia Burns
Athul Jose
Kieran McNamee
Andrew Muir
Sancia Sam
Joanne Savage
Bobby Sarvagode
Nicholas Biju Thomas
Jordan Trainer

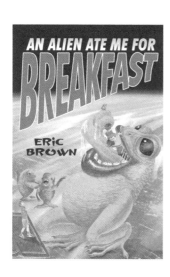

## An Alien Ate Me for Breakfast
### by
### Eric Brown

One minute, Mouse's biggest problem is the local bully. The next – he's taken away by aliens! Can Mouse and Millie find their way back to Earth – or will they be eaten for breakfast?

## A Dinosaur Ate my Socks
### by
### Eric Brown

Mouse and Millie's home-work is all about dinosaurs. So when the alien Umba-Wumba comes to visit in·his ship, the three friends go back in time to see the dinosaurs up close. But the dinosaurs get too close! Can they escape?

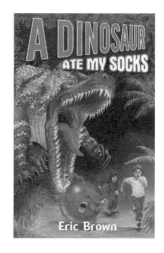

You can order these books directly from our website at
www.barringtonstoke.co.uk

## Scrum!
## by
## Tom Palmer

Steven's mad for Rugby League. His dad even reckons he'll go pro one day. Then his mum drops a bombshell. They're moving down south with her new boyfriend. To the land of Rugby Union. When the Union team wants Steven and the League scouts come calling, he faces the hardest choice of his life ...

## Ninja: First Mission
## by
## Chris Bradford

When the Grandmaster sends Taka on a special mission, this is his last chance to prove himself. But the mission is dangerous. To fail is to die, and Taka has failed before ...

You can order these books directly from our website at
www.barringtonstoke.co.uk